FRIENDS
OF ACPL

Just for

Manuel

Just for Manuel

by

DORIS HAMPTON

Illustrated by

CAROL ROGERS

STECK-VAUGHN COMPANY
AN Intext PUBLISHER
Austin, Texas

ISBN 0-8114-7722-3
Library of Congress Catalog Card Number 72-139291
Copyright © 1971 by Steck-Vaughn Company, Austin, Texas

Manuel liked school.
At school Manuel had a desk.
Manuel sat at his desk.
That was Manuel's special place.

5

At school Manuel had a place
to put his jacket.
Manuel put his jacket there.
That was Manuel's special place.

But at home there was no special
place for Manuel. His home was
in an old apartment house.

7

At home he had to share everything.
He slept in a bed with his brother
Carlos in the front room.

One day Manuel said,
"Mother, I need a place at home."

Mother was putting on her jacket.
"What place?" she asked.

Manuel stood on one foot.

"I need a place where I can put my toys."

Manuel stood on the other foot.

"I need a place just for me," he said.

Carlos and Lupe laughed.
Fernando and Juan laughed, too.
"Where will you find a place?" Carlos asked.
"Will you find a place under the bed?"

"No," said Manuel.
"There is no room under there for me."

"You keep looking," Mother said.
"You will find a place."

Manuel smiled.
Mother smiled back at him.

Then Mother went to work.
Fernando and Juan went to work, too.
Lupe went to the store.
Carlos went out to play.

Manuel said good-by.
Now there was no one else at home.

Manuel went into the kitchen.
Where could he find a place?
He looked and looked.

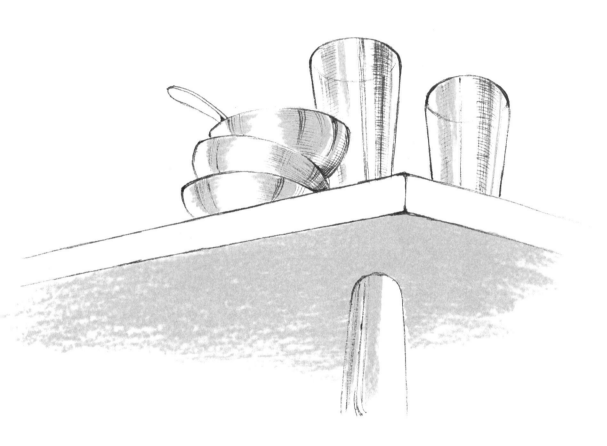

Then he saw the kitchen table.
Would that make a good place?
Manuel took the cereal box off the table.
He took the cereal bowls off the table.

21

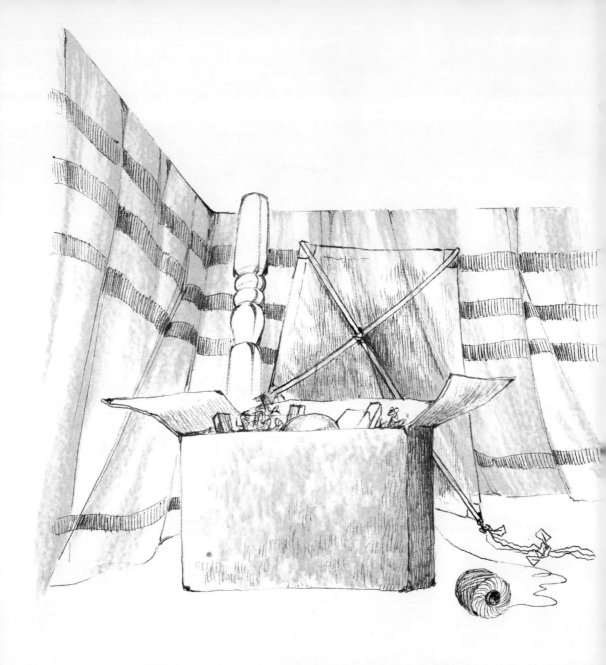

Then he took a blanket off his bed.
He put the blanket over the table.
It was a good place.

Manuel sat under the table with his
box of toys. He liked his special place.

Lupe came home from the store.
"Boo!" said Lupe.
"What are you doing?" she asked.
And she shook the blanket.

"Go away," said Manuel.
"This is my place."

"No," said Lupe.
"This is not your place.
We need the table."
And she took away his blanket.

25

Manuel went out of his apartment.
He took his box of toys into the hall.
He sat down by Mr. Grubb's door.

26

Manuel took cowboys and Indians from
his box. He played with them.
The cowboys were noisy.
The Indians were noisy.
Manuel was noisy, too.

27

Soon Mr. Grubb opened his door.
"Go away, Manuel," he said.
"I work at night. I sleep all day.
You are too noisy."
Manuel picked up his toys.

He went into his apartment.
He went into the kitchen.
Then he saw the broom closet.
Would that make a good place?

Manuel took a bucket, a broom, and a mop
from the closet. He put his box of toys
in the closet. He sat down.
The closet was not too big. It was not
too small. It was just right.

Carlos and Fernando and Juan came home.
"You found a good place," Juan said.

Mother came home. Manuel was still in
the closet.

"I found a place," Manuel told her.

31

Mother laughed.
"I knew you would," she said.
And she let him eat his supper there.